Anonymous

An Apology for the Common English Bible

Anatiposi

Anonymous

An Apology for the Common English Bible

Reprint of the original, first published in 1857.

1st Edition 2023 | ISBN: 978-3-38233-176-4

Anatiposi Verlag is an imprint of Outlook Verlagsgesellschaft mbH.

Verlag (Publisher): Outlook Verlag GmbH, Zeilweg 44, 60439 Frankfurt, Deutschland
Vertretungsberechtigt (Authorized to represent): E. Roepke, Zeilweg 44, 60439 Frankfurt, Deutschland
Druck (Print): Books on Demand GmbH, In de Tarpen 42, 22848 Norderstedt, Deutschland

AN APOLOGY

FOR THE

COMMON ENGLISH BIBLE;

AND A

REVIEW OF THE EXTRAORDINARY CHANGES

MADE IN IT BY MANAGERS

OF THE

AMERICAN BIBLE SOCIETY.

·

NO MAN PUTTETH A PIECE OF NEW CLOTH UNTO AN OLD GARMENT: FOR THAT WHICH IS PUT IN TO FILL IT UP, TAKETH FROM THE GARMENT.

S. Matt. ix. 16.

BALTIMORE:
JOSEPH ROBINSON.
NEW YORK:
DANA AND COMPANY.

1857.

PREFACE.

THE writer of the following pages has not endeavoured to conceal his religious convictions as a Churchman, but, at the same time, he has preferred to make his objections to the work set forth in the name of the American Bible Society, on grounds which he believes are common to all who believe in the Trinity and the Atonement. He writes, in no respect, as a partisan, but as one who desires to see the pure Word of GOD made the lasting possession of all his countrymen.

A. C. C.

BALTIMORE, January, 1857.

APOLOGY.

THE Holy Scriptures, as translated in the reign of king James the First, are the noblest heritage of the Anglo-Saxon race. Contemporary with the rise of colonial emigration from the great hive of parent life and enterprise, the English Bible, of that epoch, would seem designed, by Providence, to be the parting blessing of the Mother of Nations, to her adventurous progeny. Itself the product of long years of fidelity to the great Charter of man's salvation, it represented to the emigrant, not alone the love and care of the Church of that particular age; but it came to him, hallowed with the memory of a long line of witnesses, to whom he owed it under GOD. It was the work, in some degree, of all, who, in the successive stages of England's growth and development, had contributed to that great principle of the Anglican Reformation, that the Bible, with all its precious promises, is, by covenant with GOD, the rightful treasure of every Christian man, and of every Christian child. It was the Bible of Adhelm and Bede and Ælfric and of Alfred; of Stephen Langton and Rolle of Hampole; of Wiclif and Tindal and Coverdale and Cranmer and Parker, and of all the noble army of Marian Martyrs. Finally, it was the Bible which had been winnowed from whatever was unsubstantial in the fruits of all their labours, and which combined the merits of all; it was the finest of the wheat. When it appeared, Shakespeare and Spenser had written in poetry, and Hooker in prose, and Milton was just born. The English language was in its prime and purity; its wells were undefiled. As yet, there were no developed schisms in the great family; recusants were few, and non-conformists were not yet dissenters. The great work was, itself, an Irenicum, and for a time, it seemed as if the spreading plague of religious dissension might be stayed. If not, it remained to be seen, as it yet does, whether this golden casket might not contain the elixir of renovation, and prove, in the end, the "healer of the breach," of the common family to which the English language is the mother-tongue. It went abroad, in every adventurer's chest, the talisman of his ancestral faith, and the keepsake of home affection. It went to Jamestown, and it went to Plymouth Rock. It was read by the camp-fire of Smith, on the Virginia river, and by the winter fireside of the Fathers of New England. There was at least one thing held in common by both these colonies; and, whatever may have been the discontent of the Puritan, he could not open his Bible without a kindly thought towards the Church of England, as a Mother, whose breasts were flowing with the milk of God's Word, even though her hands were employed in chastisement and discipline. "For myself," said Robinson, the leader of the Puritan emigration to Holland, "I believe with my heart, and profess with my tongue, that I have one and the same faith, hope, spirit, baptism, and LORD, which I had in the Church of England, and none other." So, on the deck of the Arabella, Winthrop and his associates wrote their famous letter, "calling the Church of England their dear Mother," and declaring that they could not part from "their native country, where she specially resideth, without much sadness of heart, and tears in their eyes; ever acknowledging that such hope and part as they had obtained in the common salvation, they had received in her bosom, and sucked it from her breasts."

And now, after two hundred years of the sending forth of colonies, the Anglo-Saxon people dwell in every latitude and longitude; they mingle their blood with other races, and yet remain one with the parent stock. Time, indeed, is working changes; and far-severed branches of the same original family must have their own household feelings, and immediate ties of home. It is not altogether true, alas! that this mighty people have all "one LORD, one faith, one baptism." If it were so, the world would be their easy conquest for the Cross. They do not pray the same prayers, nor with one heart and one mouth, confess the same "form of sound words." But as yet, over and above the common spirit of their laws, they hold fast the great Charter, from which their free laws have proceeded; they possess the same Bible.

Can it be necessary to argue that no one can inflict a graver wound on the unity of the race, and on all the sacred interests which depend on that unity, under GOD, than by tampering with the English Bible ? By the acclamation of the universe, it is the most faultless version of the Scriptures that ever existed in any tongue. To complain of its trifling blemishes, is to complain of the sun for its spots. Whatever may be its faults, they are less evil, in every way, than would be the evils sure to arise from any attempt to eradicate them ; and where there is so much of wheat, the few tares may be allowed to stand till the end of the world. Two centuries, complete, have identified even its slightest peculiarities with the whole literature, poetry, prose, and science, as well as with the entire thought and theology of those ages, and the time, to all appearance, is forever past, when any alteration can be made in it, without a shock to a thousand holy things, and to the pious sensibilities of millions.

The care with which the Hebrews guarded every jot and tittle of their Scriptures was never reproved by our SAVIOUR. It is our duty and interest to imitate them in the jealousy with which GOD's Holy Word is kept in our own language. Even the antiquated words of the English Bible will never become obsolete, while they are preserved in the amber of its purity ; and there, they have a precious beauty and propriety which they would lack elsewhere. The language lives there in its strength, as in a citadel, and knows no damage, while it keeps that house like a strong man armed. He who would rub off those graceful marks of age which adorn our version, vulgarizes and debases that venerable dignity with which the first ideas of religion came to the youthful mind and heart from the old and hoary Bible.

But it is a graver thought, that no individual, and no set of individuals, can leave even a mark upon the Bible, in these days, without disfiguring and injuring it, in the estimation of the great majority of readers. No commission from the Queen, no concurrence of the Universities, no act of Convocation of the Church of England herself, could make any change involving matter of faith, opinion, or even of taste, that could be accepted so universally, as is the work in its integrity, as it now exists, petty faults and infinite merits together. The best and the most that can be done, even in England, is to ensure the strict preservation of the text and its accessories, as they are according to the present standards. For, granting all that can be said against the present translation, the question is, can any other that can now be made, become what this is, to the world? It will not do for England to take an insular view of this question, nor for us to take an American one. It is of the utmost consequence, that the whole Anglo-Saxon people should have one Bible, as one GOD. It is of vast consequence to Christendom, that there should not be a multiplication of Bibles, every sect setting forth its own. It is of the highest importance, as every thoughtful Christian will admit, that the unhappy divisions which now exist, should not be made manifold more and greater, as would certainly be the case, should this idea of sectarian Bibles gain the ascendant. For

2

who does not feel it all important that Christians should re-unite, and not increase their quarrels? Who does not deplore the existing estrangements among professed disciples of CHRIST? Who would not suffer the loss of many things for the sake of bringing all "who love the LORD JESUS CHRIST in sincerity," into one accord, and one mind, that all might strive, together, for the faith of the Gospel!

The movement, in England, which has made some little stir in Parliament, in behalf of a new translation, seems to have been set on foot by parties confessedly averse to the great doctrinal truths of the Gospel. It is significant, that the Edinburgh Review, in a late article of distinctly latitudinarian character, has pronounced in favour of the experiment. But even the Edinburgh Review, with all its Scottish prejudices and non-ecclesiastical sympathies, deprecates any private enterprise of the kind, and insists that it must proceed from the Church of England, and by a commission from the Queen, such as performed the original work. With regard to voluntary Societies, while it opines that they will not be deterred from a similar undertaking, it says, forcibly, however, that "this is an evil which we most earnestly deprecate;" and it adds: "With all our anxiety to witness the issue of a corrected translation of the Sacred Scriptures, . . . we should deeply regret to find it attempted without authority, at the expense of an unlearned Society, and under the direction of an anonymous editor. The Holy Bible, on the right understanding of which the salvation of us all depends, ought not to *be thus lightly and irreverently dealt by.*"

Now it is certain, that the millions of Anglo-Saxon Christians, who belong to the Anglican Communion, would not take the amended Bible on any lower authority than that of such a Commission as the reviewer suggests : but would they accept it, even on such authority? Or can it be imagined that others would do so, English or Americans, even if the Churchman should? It is evident that the proposal of the reviewer is based upon ideas of Lord Palmerston's continued reign, and of the appointment of such "erudite persons" as the latitudinarian Mr. Jowett. But the Church of England would never submit to such a Commission, nor would any other Christians who believe in Christ Crucified, and in the plenary inspiration of the Sacred Oracles.

We believe, therefore, that the time has gone by for the radical improvement of the English Bible, even in England. But if it cannot be done, at the fountain, in the mother land, it surely cannot be done elsewhere : for this river of Paradise is "parted from thence, and become into four heads," in the four quarters of the globe, so that nothing that is done in any one branch can possibly flow to all. There is certainly no possibility that the plan suggested by the Edinburgh Review could be satisfactorily carried out in our generation ; and its proposal, that the commission should be a perpetual one, is a suggestion of such unbounded change, as makes one shudder. Every generation has its fashions ; and the Bible, set and set again, according to prevailing whims, would become as untrustworthy as an old town-clock, continually corrected by private watches. It must be remembered, that critical Bibles and commentaries, professedly such, will constantly be coming forth, from competent scholars, and will be always at hand for those who need them. It is only of the standard that we are speaking. Let pious men multiply their contributions to this sacred wealth of nations: let even revised translations be put forth, for private use and study; and, if ever, by the disappearance of heresies and schisms, the good day should arrive, when a few wholesome emendations might pass into the standard, as by acclamation, then, but not till then, in the LORD's name, let it be done.

If these sober views of the reverend sanctity, and inestimable worth, of our common English Bible, are not unreasonable, it would seem to follow that nothing less than a very general public movement could justify any private association, or any combination of individuals, in an attempt to alter the standard for a whole people, speaking the English tongue. Strange that the present moment is witness to two such attempts, nevertheless, on the part of voluntary Societies in America! That any man, or set of men, however respectable in their spheres of private usefulness, should propose themselves as the competent emendators of such a standard, or dream of producing a Bible for common use, that should unite the suffrages of their fellow Christians, and supersede the time-honored version in its integrity, would seem to prove that nothing is too holy for the hand of rash innovation, or too high for the adventure of presumptuous experiment:

> " As if religion were intended
> For nothing else but to be mended !"

Refined gold must be gilded, and the lily painted; and if possible, the very lights of heaven would be tinkered and repaired, by the wild conceit of the times: but, to see good and pious men, touched with the same enthusiasm which infects the unthinking and irreligious, is indeed deplorable. How melancholy the exhibition which the worthy, but mistaken, projectors of the " New Baptist Version" have made of themselves and their cause; and how sad the spectacle presented by the " American Bible Society," in its half-way adventure towards the same conclusion!

Of that Society, in its original plan and conception, I desire to speak with all respect. Of its present constituency, I would scarcely speak with less. I believe it embraces thousands who have been, in no wise, parties to the exploits of its managers, which I find almost unknown as matter of fact, and quite unsuspected, as to character and extent. Though the writer has never been able to confide in the practical wisdom of the Society, or in the elements of its Constitution, so far as to become one of its members, he profoundly sympathizes with its professed object; and yields the sincerest homage to the example and judgment of many, his superiors in years and dignity, who have heretofore confided in its management, and regarded its fidelity to the declared purposes of its founders, as unimpeachable. And, certainly, so long as the Society continued to supply the million with the virgin Scriptures, he never could have supposed it his duty to add another voice to the warnings, which, at the very outset of the Society's career, denounced its ultimate tendencies as dangerous to truth, on the ground of its compromises with error. But I believe those tendencies have now developed into manifest proclivities towards a surrender of great Christian principles. For more than thirty years, the Society is said to have celebrated its great anniversary festivals, in the presence of hundreds of professed ministers of CHRIST, without a prayer for His blessing, or an ascription to the glory of the Holy Trinity; and that, confessedly, on the ground of the radical differences among its constituents, as to the very nature of GOD, and the proper manner of invoking His adorable name. While proposing a practical union of Christians, such as the Word and Sacraments, ordained of CHRIST Himself, are pronounced incapable of effecting, it has resulted in new divisions, and in the production of a rival "American Bible Society," and a rival version,—on the part of the Baptists. Can such an association be a safe " witness and keeper of Holy Writ ?" It has answered the question, by making itself a manufacturer of alloy, and debasing the very standard it is pledged to circulate in its integrity. It already circulates a Bible which justifies the worst "prophecies which went before on it," from the lips of Bishop Hobart; and, yet, no one can examine this new standard, and the principles on which it has been produced, without seeing that, if once admitted, it must prove the precursor of changes the most thorough, and the most fatal to orthodoxy. What has been done already, should it prove acceptable, will authorize the further amendment of a thousand texts, and the entire subversion of the standard in common use. And even if it proceeds no further, it degrades Holy Scripture in the popular estimation: it destroys the feeling, so healthful and so prevalent, that the Bible is a book above change, and too holy to be subjected to experiments; and, that wholesome habit of confidence in CHRIST, as the alpha and omega of both Testaments, which the old Bible, with its quaint summaries, generated so naturally in the heart of youth, must entirely disappear, under its widely different spirit. Should it become the Bible of the American people, a cold, modernized, and (to the man of feeling) a vulgarized work will have supplanted the Bible which we have known from childhood, and which has made so many "wise unto salvation." But I hope the Christians of America are not prepared for such a change; and I believe that many members of the Bible Society deplore and feel the injury already done, as much as I do, and are as anxious that it should be arrested before it goes further.

In concluding these introductory remarks, it may be well to introduce a letter of the present Primate of all England, who is universally revered for his piety, and who will not be accused of prelatical bigotry by any party. It was written to the Rev. Mr. Mason, of Maryland, as Chairman of a Committee of the General Convention on the Standard Bible of the Anglo-American Church ; and it would seem, accordingly, that there is a recognized Standard Text in the Mother Country, to which every motive would lead us to conform as closely as possible.

LAMBETH, *April 17th*, 1851.

DEAR SIR,—I am happy to have it in my power to answer your letter of inquiry concerning the text of the Bible.

During the years 1834, 1835 and 1836, the delegates of the Oxford and the Syndics of the Cambridge press had a long and elaborate correspondence on the state of the text of the Bible as then printed, and until then there had been much inaccuracy. A correct text, according to the edition of 1611, was then adopted, both in the Oxford and Cambridge Bibles. The Secretary of the Society for Promoting Christian Knowledge has furnished me with the following statement from Mr. Combe, the superintendent of the Oxford press :—

'The text of all the Oxford editions of the Bible is now the same, and is in conformity with the edition of 1611, which is, and has been for many years, adopted for the standard text. The medium quarto book is stereotyped, which protects it from casual errors ; and having been long in use without the detection of any error, I have reason to think that it may be considered as perfect as a book can be, and may therefore be fairly received as the Standard Book of the Society.'

It is a most gratifying thought, that our English Bible should be circulated over your vast continent, and that our native language should be employed as the vehicle of Eternal Truth to an increasing multitude of readers ; and we may justly pray, that the purity which is secured to the text, may be extended also to the doctrines gathered from the text and propounded to the hearers of the Word.

It gives me much pleasure to have had this opportunity of communicating with an American brother, and I remain, Rev. Sir, your faithful servant, J. B. CANTUAR.

Rev. HENRY M. MASON.

The American Bible Society, instituted in 1816, has always professed that "the SOLE OBJECT" of its existence is "the encouragement of a wider circulation of the Holy Scriptures without note or comment;" and that "the only copies in the English language to be circulated by the Society shall be of the version *now* (1816) *in common use.*" To auxiliary societies it has proposed as a corresponding article of Constitution, that their object should be "to promote the circulation of the Holy Scriptures, without note or comment, and in English those of the commonly received version."[a]

Could any human being have imagined that a society, endowed and enriched by the gifts and bequests of pious men for this *sole object*, could ever have supposed itself authorized to undertake the work of thoroughly criticising and revising the received version, and setting it forth anew, not merely amended IN THE TEXT, divested of its archaisms and Græcisms, furnished with sundry new marginal comments, and purged of many of its old marginal notes and references ; but also furnished with a new system of summaries or headings, containing the most pregnant comment, in its unity of cast and conception ; and, as compared with what it supplants, amounting to a severe censure on the old Bible, and on the general tone of Evangelical religion by which it is characterized? Such a sweeping work has been achieved, nevertheless, by Managers of the Society, and is now the standard, in which it glories, and which, for the present, it circulates exclusively.

[a] See Annual Reports, &c.

3

I say *for the present;* for who shall say how long the
managers of such a Society, growing richer and richer
every year, and finding employment for a body of men,
not by any means too small for its reasonable operations, will be content with such meagre preliminaries?
Thirty years more, and another generation may see a
new experiment, under the sanction of this, which will
be carried further; and a vast body of Neologists may
entirely control the work of a new translation. Expe-
rience demonstrates that I am not a gratuitous alarmist.
While I am writing these pages, a respectable newspaper, of the "Reformed Dutch Communion," records the
deplorable success of such a scheme, in the bosom of
the Fatherland of that interesting branch of the Con-
tinental Reformation. Hear its unexceptionable testimony! It says:

"The National Church of Holland, the descendant of the Old Reformed Church of Dort, has, it is true, still its old orthodox standards;
but by additional regulations the Synod has deprived them of their
binding power, in consequence of which Rationalism and Unitarianism
have, in the course of the last fifty years, seized almost the whole of
the clergy. The Synod recently by an official verdict virtually declared, that ministers who hold Unitarian views are legal office-bearers
of the Church. Of her 1500 ministers, not more than a hundred are
known as maintaining Evangelical truth; and the Synod *has resolved
to publish a new translation of the Bible,* which (as the committee and
translators consist, almost without exception, of Unitarians) will doubt-
less favor their views—and thus *the faith of the people, sustained by
the old Dutch translation, one of the best in Europe, will be still further
undermined."*

I trust such a fact may beget a willingness, on the
part of some, otherwise prejudiced in favor of anything

which may proceed from a source so respectable as the Managing Committee of the American Bible Society, to bear with me, as I proceed to examine, in a spirit of candid inquiry, and without injustice to what is good in their work, this novel and amended " Standard Bible." I have before me their own Report, printed in 1852. I have been familiar with their work since 1853, when my attention was called to it by a respected brother in the Ministry, who thought it might deserve to be made the standard of the Church to which we both belong. But I find that the fact is not generally known, even among members of the Society, that such a Report exists, or that the extensive changes of which it speaks, have been made. I have hoped that some one, more immediately interested, might offer remonstrances. I find that many are anxious to know what has been done ; and circumstances have forced me, reluctantly, to make this attempt to enlighten them.

It is justly urged, that the committee who are responsible for the new Bible, consists of highly respectable men, and men of known piety and learning. But it may be answered, as forcibly, that were it otherwise, it would hardly be worth while to take any notice of their performance. It is not my good fortune to be known to any of them personally, save only the venerable Dr. Turner, of the General Theological Seminary. But every one knows, at least by reputation, the learned and laborious Dr. Robinson, whose name and scholarship are an honour to his country. I am not aware that any other members of the Committee are distinguished

as Biblical critics; and lively as is my sense of the regard which is due to eminent worth and piety, I cannot
see that anything is added to the dignity or strength of
the Committee, by any of its members, whose distinc-
tion lies in other walks of life, or in other departments
of science. The strength of a chain is not increased by
its inferior links, however numerous or polished they
may be; and the real claim of the Committee upon our
deference seems to me to reside in the fact that it com-
prehends the names of Drs. Turner and Robinson.
How much of the labour that has been expended on the
work has been contributed by these distinguished scholars, it may be well to inquire, but my review of the
work is based on the postulate, that no private criticism, however respectable, has a right to alter the Standard English Bible.

For if it requires some confidence in the sanctity, as
well as justice, of one's course, to criticise the doings
of Drs. Turner and Robinson, let me direct attention to
the assurance which it requires in any man to overrule
and "go behind"[a] those giants of Scriptural scholarship,
the translators of the Bible. If my review should, by
any, be construed as reflecting upon two of the wor-
thiest scholars of our times, I hope it may be remembered, that it is rather a defence of forty great scholars
of the old time, whose reputation and labours have received the homage of men of learning for more than
two centuries complete. Let me begin by a reference
to the favourite Dr. Reynolds, called by the Committee

[a] See the Report of Committee on Versions, p. 19.

" the leader of the Puritans." Such an epithet does
little justice to the friend of Jewell and Hooker, who
lived and died in the Communion of the Church of England, ate of her bread, officiated in her vestments, and
knelt at her altars, and whose last breath was a request
for the priestly absolution, contained in her office for
the visitation of the sick. "The memory and reading
of that man were near to a miracle," according to Bishop Hall; and according to Fuller, his non-conformity
amounted only to a charity for those whose scruples
were not his own. But who shall compare with the
great Bishop Andrewes, to whose virtue even Milton
could not grudge a tribute:

> At te præcipue luxi, dignissime præsul,
> Wintoniæque olim gloria magna tuæ:

and whose private prayers were written and uttered
" with strong crying and tears" before GOD, in the
Greek tongue? I will not presume upon the ignorance
of my readers, in saying more of such men, nor in
dwelling on the praises of Saravia, the bosom-friend
and counsellor of Hooker; of Bedwell, "the industrious
and thrice-learned;" of Livlie, of Chaderton, of Sir
Henry Savile, and others their equals in learning, and
their worthy associates. But let me add, at least, as
giving an idea of the varied learning, theological opin-
ions, and tastes, which had room to operate in the production of our Bible, the names of Bishops Overall,
Barlow, Miles Smith and Bilson, and the Calvinistic
Archbishop Abbot. A biographical history of all who

had part in the Translation, is a desideratum, and might be an effectual antidote to the itch for superseding their work, which seems to trouble so many in our days. While, then, for myself, I should feel profoundly unworthy to advance a critical opinion, contrary to those of the two eminent linguists engaged in the production of this new standard, I cannot blush for my presumption, in defending, even against their amendments, the work of those great men, concerning whom their contemporary, Fuller, says, so eloquently, " Wheresoever the Bible shall be preached, or read, in the whole world, there shall also this that they have done be told in memorial of them."

It certainly was due to the memory of such men, that no inferior hands should be allowed to tamper with their work. A Michael Angelo might be trusted to restore a broken work of Phidias, but who would not prefer the antique, with all its blemishes, to the mendings of any secondary genius ? It becomes important, then, to inquire, how far the emendation of this precious work was entrusted to Drs. Turner and Robinson, and whether their names are more than a nominal guarantee of the sound judgment, taste, and scholarship employed in the performance. I have closely scrutinized the Report, to find out, especially, whether Dr. Turner has had more than a subordinate hand in it : and while I feel much relieved, by finding that he has lent little more than his honored name to the enterprise, I am amazed at the discovery that Dr. Robinson, the only remaining critic, has had a merely secondary share in it. The work is primarily the product of another hand: the hand not of a retired and studious scholar; but of a respectable Presbyterian pastor, immersed in professional cares, and consequently labouring under almost every disadvantage as an emendator. This fact disarms criticism so far as relates to this party, and excuses the bungling which is apparent, even from the Report of the Committee; but it does not excuse the Managers from the charge of having committed a work of magnitude and importance, to hands from which no reflecting man would willingly accept an amended Bible.

I have arrived at these conclusions from a comparison of several parts of the Report. That Dr. Turner's responsibility is nominal, appears from the fact that while divers minor celebrities receive each his modicum of praise, "according to his several ability," no such praise is accorded to the distinguished ability of this eminent Professor. His name seems only to be used as a compliment to the Church of which he is so bright an ornament. Nor can I perceive that the erudition of Dr. Robinson is any great warrant for confidence. He seems to have served merely as one of a Sub-Committee, which met "once in each week and sometimes oftener" to review the labours of the principal party to the enterprise, "the Collator" himself. This worthy gentleman deserves no small praise, so far as his "Collation" may be regarded as private study. It pains me to seem censorious, when speaking of his long and careful devotion to the duty assigned him. He reports hardly less than 24,000 variations in the "text and punctuation of the six copies compared;" but we are consoled by the assertion that "of all this great number, there is not one which mars the integrity of the text, or affects any doctrine, or precept of the Bible." Such an assurance would have been very valuable from a Sir William Jones, or from Dr. Blaney. But we mean no disrespect when we say that the Report does not profoundly impress us with confidence, when it gives us this verdict, upon his own toils, and with respect to 24,000 variations, from the " Pastor of the First Presbyterian Church in Williamsburgh, N. Y." The fault is not his, but comes home to the Managers. If the work was to be done at all, surely they owed it to themselves, and to the good sense of the nation, to commit it to a Commission of professional scholars, of universally approved erudition, and free from other cares. Why was not this course taken? I can think of only one probable reason. They may have felt that they had no constitutional right to expend the funds of the contributors on critical labours ; and hence they may have found themselves forced to accept the voluntary and gratuitous aid of the first good and pious man, whose zeal and diligence were sufficient to stimulate him to the undertaking. All honor to the spirit of such a man : but who would not prefer the unaltered work of Dr. Blaney, of whom even the Report bears witness that his attempt to restore the text to its original purity, " was successfully accomplished, *to as great a degree as can well be expected in any work of like extent ?*"

It would seem, then, that after printing for thirty
years a certain Bible, professing to be according to the
version in common use, the "Committee on Versions"
has furnished the Society and the world with another;
that this other is made the standard, and that, to it, all
the Society's English Bibles must hereafter be conformed. To excuse this substitution, much waste of
words, and of labour with pen and ink, has been made,
in comparing divers Bibles, and in shewing up their
faults. But what have we to do with Scotch and
American reprints, when we all know where to find an
English Standard Bible? There is no need of learned
and antiquarian research: for the question is one of
plain common sense. We will concede, that for thirty
years the Society had fulfilled its pledge, and circulated
an unexceptionable Bible, according to the standard "in
common use," in 1816. Its fidelity in so doing had con-
ciliated a great degree of popular confidence and favour.
No one found fault with the trifling "note and comment" contained in the old headings. They were taken
as part and parcel of the work. A whole generation
passed away without any one's dreaming that there was
anything contrary to the Society's object, in the circulation of the Bible, as they found it, entire. The Society
could not change its position with reference to these
summaries, without stultifying itself. Still, if the decay
of old orthodoxy demanded the removal of landmarks,
which their fathers had set, the Managers had one
course before them, to which no objection could have
been made on the score of their Constitutional pledges.

4

They might have resolved on the circulation of the Standard Text only; and their Bibles might have followed the usual pocket form, in the entire omission of the headings. Much as some members of the Society would have regretted even such a concession to the religious dyspepsia which happens to be fashionable, for the time, I believe no one would have remonstrated; and good men generally, though they might have received new impressions of the untrustworthiness of a Management unable to hold its ground, and to resist the beginnings of innovation, might have rejoiced in the multiplication of sound copies of GOD's Word, and would have been far from anticipating the worst, or raising the voice of censure and alarm.

It is the tendency of all human institutions to corrupt themselves, especially when they have begun to be rich. The American Bible Society, in its new palace, and surrounded by the excitement of the great moneyed mart of this hemisphere, waxes fat, like Jeshurun, and like him, begins to kick. Its strength would have been to sit still. If it could have resisted the temptation to do something more than was given it to do, no one would have ventured to inquire as to the propriety of its joining house to house, and multiplying its presses and diversifying its operations. True, its Constitution says nothing about all this: but then the good-natured public supposes all this to be necessary to the *circulating* of the Holy Scriptures, and possibly it is so. But the possession of such facilities for original work is a great stimulant to the undertaking of large enterprises. That such a Body

should be content to circulate a Bible conformed to any
standard "in common use," seems beneath its dignity.
A modest experiment is resolved on, which grows less
modest as it proceeds. A collation of versions is un-
dertaken in 1847, and a highly respectable Presbyterian minister of Williamsburgh is appointed the "Collator," in 1848. The laborious employment of this
gentleman and divers assistants, for nineteen months,
results in a thorough revision, aided by an entire new
set of stereotype plates, which would seem to have
been duplicated, and to have been made before the
work was approved by the "Board of Managers," or
by any other authority than that of a Sub-Committee,
of the Committee, by them appointed. The final report of their work seems to have been adopted by the
"Board of Managers," May 1, 1851; but even then the
standard was not out of press, and was adopted as such,
much as the Sixtine Vulgate was by the Council of
Trent, before any one knew what it might be.

To this new Bible, I desire to do the fullest justice.
It is a beautiful specimen of typographical art, and is
furnished so cheaply, that had it been the good old
Bible, according to the former standards of the Society,
it would have been a boon to the nation. As the case
is, however, its fair type, and its great cheapness, are so
much the worse. They tend to push all the old Bibles
out of the market, and to make it difficult for any one
to find such a Bible as the Society was founded to circulate. No one, to whom his Bible has been for years
a constant companion, can give it a critical glance

without saying, involuntarily, "how is this?" It presents an altered look : an appearance of elaborate deformity, as when a dear old face comes before one for the first time, with an entire set of artificial teeth, of which the very beauty is shocking. The old pearls, with all their blemishes, were better-looking; and there is something foolish in the expression which the new decorations give to an otherwise grave and decorous countenance. So here, the loss of the old running heads, and the supply of new ones; and much more the supply of the new summaries, or arguments, are severely felt. New wine has been poured into the old bottles ; and, on every account, one feels that " the old is better."

Let us examine the Society's own 8vo. Bible of 1850, which was taken as " the basis for corrections," and compare, with it, their new work, as expounded by the Report aforementioned. One naturally asks, to begin with, what was the need of any meddling with an old standard ; and after thirteen pages of utterly irrelevant talk, we find that there was absolutely none. The Report finally reaches several " results," of which not one is of the slightest practical importance, save only the last, which was sufficiently understood before by every tolerably informed Bible reader, and which is as follows :

" That the revision of Dr. Blaney, made by collating the then current editions of Oxford and Cambridge with those of 1611 and 1701, had for its main object to restore the text of the English Bible to its original purity ; and that this was successfully accomplished, to as great a degree as can well be expected in any work of like extent."

Now this result is of great importance. It admits the existence of a competent standard, in its original purity, made to the Society's hand. There remained to the Board, then, the simple duty of importing as accurate a "Blaney" as could be found, and ordering that future editions should be faithfully conformed to it, except in the case of any manifest printer's errour. What other course could have been anticipated?

But here the Report flies back from its result, and raises a cloud of dust about the many bad editions that exist in America and elsewhere. It treats us to the following entertaining facts, among others:

" There exists, for instance, the ' Vinegar Edition,' so called, printed at Oxford in 1717, in two volumes folio; in which the word ' vinegar' is put for ' vineyard' in Luke 13, 7.

" In like manner, in several editions between 1638 and 1685, in Acts 6, 3, where the appointment of seven deacons is spoken of, the reading is changed from ' whom we may appoint' to ' whom ye may appoint.' This variation has sometimes been charged upon the Independents, as intentional on their part; but as it first appeared in the Cambridge edition in 1638, and is not noted again until the time of the restoration, when it is found in the copies of Cambridge, London and Edinburgh, this charge would seem to be without foundation; and the error, probably, was merely one of the press.

" In one American edition, in Gal. 4, 27, the verse is thus printed: ' For it is written, Rejoice, thou barren that bearest not; break forth and cry, thou that travailest not: for the desolate hath many more children than she which hath an hundred;' so printed instead of ' husband.' "

But what has all this to do with the fact that the "Blaney" Bible is a sound and good one? It seems to be lugged in to disguise the "result" which had been

attained, and to account for the very solemn intro-
duction of the simple fact, which is reached on page
15th, that the Committee has another standard, and a
very different one, to account for. This they begin to
talk about, as follows :

" The attention of the Committee was first drawn to the subject
under consideration, at their meeting, Oct. 6th, 1847. At that time
Mr. Secretary Brigham communicated to them, that the Superintendent
of printing found many discrepancies still existing between our different editions of the English Bible ; and also between our editions and
those issued by the British and Foreign Bible Society. Several specimens of such discrepancies were exhibited to the Committee, relating
mostly to the use of *Italic words*, *Capital Letters*, and *the Article a* or
an. After consideration, the Committee referred the matter to the
Board of Managers for counsel and direction."

One would think the Committee might have answered, that it was desirable that the best of the editions
should be followed, and that the articles *a* or *an* were
safe enough, in that case, as they had been for the past
thirty years. But, on the contrary, after the appointment of the Collator, they give him nine rules of their
own, of which several are wise and unobjectionable, but
of which others are, to say the least, gratuitous. The
Collator was ordered, by rule 6th, to correct the text
by uniformly using *an* "before all vowels and dipthongs
not pronounced as consonants, and also before *h*, silent
or unaccented," using the form *a* in all other cases. By
rule 4th, the concurrence and uniformity of the four
English copies (the fifth was Scotch) selected as standards, were to be followed, *unless otherwise specially
ordered by the Committee !* By rule 3d, the Collator

was to compare " the *Orthography, Capital Letters, Words in Italic, and Punctuation*," of the Society's former edition, with these standards : but the Report adds with *naïveté*, in a parenthesis,—" To these were added, *in practice*, the contents of the chapters, and the running heads !" A pregnant parenthesis, it must be allowed ! We shall see what it brings forth. On page 19th, we reach the " Specimens of variations," (these words, printed in capitals,) and of " *the changes which they have seen fit to adopt both in the Text and its Accessories.*" This about *changes*, is printed in such a manner as to attract no attention. But we come at last to the (I) TEXT, under its proper head; and here we find that the Committee have desired to restore the English Version to its original purity, "saving the necessary changes of orthography, *and other like variations which would assuredly be acceptable to the translators themselves, were they living at the present day !*" Here one asks, naturally, why were even these orthographical changes *necessary?* Why is it necessary to spell *errour* without the *u*, which belongs to it by every law of etymology, seeing our Latin comes to us through the Normans? Why is it necessary to modernize the antique spellings which one loves occasionally to meet, amid the leaves of his Bible, and which the humblest reader is willing to see there, though not in his newspaper? And then who can speak for the venerable translators, when we are assured what they would have done had they been living now? The signers of the report are all most respectable men ; I esteem them highly for their talents and Christian virtues : but I do not think they can be quite sure what Bishop Andrewes and others, almost his equals in learning and piety, would have done in 1851, to amend their labours of three centuries ago. I am hardly less surprised at what follows :—" The Committee have had no authority, and no desire, to *go behind the translators ;* nor in any respect to touch the original version of the text ; *unless* in cases of evident inadvertence, or inconsistency, open and manifest to all." Now, I ask, what have the Committee to do with the *translation,* and its inconsistencies, and inadvertencies ? Is it the *sole object* of the Society to improve the version ? Is not its business solely with the inadvertencies of printers, and the variations of the press ? Is not this " going behind the translators"—or, in other words, stepping into the work of 1611,—strange business for those whose *sole object* is to " circulate," not amend, the version in common use in 1816 ?

They proceed to report several emendations " on the very threshold." In principle, the specimens exhibit a dangerous precedent : but in themselves are harmless. The beautiful variety which occurs in one of the *refrains* or *antiphons*, of the Canticles, disappears, however, on insufficient grounds. " I charge you, oh ye daughters of Jerusalem. . . . . that ye stir not up, nor awake my love till *He* please :" this (*He* for *she*) has been often used, of our Lord's entombment, in a poetical way with great effect ; but it is no more to appear in the English Bible, as published by the Society. They say " these instances have *of course* been corrected according to the

Hebrew." But, why, *of course?* Admitting that it should be so corrected, is this work of "correcting, by the Hebrew," any legitimate part of the Society's business? If so, where is it to end? And what becomes of its "*sole* object?" This is a very serious matter. In doing a like work for the Church of Rome, old Sixtus V. could trust nobody's hand but his own; and miserable as was the botch he made of it, it is honourable to that corrupt Church, that the work of correcting her standard Bible was committed to the very highest authority she acknowledged. Are we less scrupulous as to GOD's Word?

To say nothing of the other instances, " the Committee *have not hesitated* to insert the definite article," in Matt. xii. 41, where "all the copies read *shall rise up in judgment,* making it read, *shall rise up in the judgment.*" But if all the copies read " shall rise *up* in judgment," why is *up* left out, and *the* put in: for so it is in the Society's Bible, in the text referred to? I suspect the *up* is an " inadvertence" in the Report; but there is certainly no call for this petty amendment, on any ground. If such things are done in cases of slight importance, they may hereafter be done in cases of vast importance, and no scholar need be reminded of the very great consequence of the Greek article in Scripture.

By the way, to show how quick they are in England to note such changes as are here made light of, a change lately crept into one of the Cambridge Octavo Bibles, in the text of II Chronicles, *xxi.* 2. It was the substitution of *Judah* for *Israel,* which is plainly required by

5

the context, and by the Hebrew. But other editions have always had it otherwise, and inquiry was immediately set on foot as to the author of the novelty. I marvel that it does not appear in the work of this Committee, for by their scheme, it ought to do so, and their rules cannot long be satisfied with instances "so few and far between."

Returning to *orthography*, it is pleasing to learn that "the Committee entertain a reverence for the antique forms of words and orthography in the Bible, where they do not conflict with a clear understanding of the sense." They add, moreover, most forcibly, "It is such forms, in a measure, which impart an air of dignity and venerableness to our version." Why then, (if *hoised up the mainsail*, and *graffed in*, are retained, on such grounds,) are some fifty capricious alterations introduced? Why need *carcases* become carc*asses?* Who does not love the sound word *throughly*, in its place, now and then, and not always *thoroughly?* For one, in the Bible, I would still see *musick* and not *music*, and *cuckow* instead of the modern *cuckoo*. Why change a sacred text, in such a fanciful way? They tell us that "by far the greater portion of the readers of the English Bible are unlearned persons and children, and it is *essential* to remove everything, in the mere form, which may become to any a stumbling-block in the way of the right and prompt understanding of GOD's Holy Word." But will any old lady suffer from not getting a "prompt understanding" of the sense, when she reads that Jacob's rams were ring*straked* and not ring*streaked?* Or cannot any child understand the word *horse bridles* in the Apocalypse? Yet the Committee mend such petty phrases, and fortify their reading—*horses' bridles*—with the important assurance that it is "so in the Greek."

Again, why reduce the *utter court* in Ezekiel, to the *outer court?* We shall have, next time, "the *utter*most parts of the earth" modernized into "the *outer*most." One is hardly ready to bid farewell to the old form *lift* (instead of *lifted,*) still familiar, in the Psalter, to every Churchman; and as for *astonied*, who would drop it in the narrative of Daniel? Yet it goes. Even the Edinburgh Review cannot but blame Dr. Blaney for the few changes he made in 1769; and the reviewer actually pauses in the full tide of his grumbling against the Received Text, to say of these emendations, that "it was a bold and hardly warrantable measure, though it extended no farther than printing *more* for *moe; midst* for *mids; owneth* for *oweth; jaws* for *chaws; alien* for *alient*, &c." If it was *bold* to make these changes in the spelling of words so common, as almost to require relief from such disguise, what shall be said of far more radical emendations made by persons occupying a purely private position, as compared with the semi-authoritative one of Dr. Blaney?

But another old landmark is removed by the petty and pedantic alteration of the old forms, which add a superfluous *s* to the Hebrew plural. Who does not love the quaintness of the forms *anakims, cherubims*, &c.? It is familiar in Shakspeare, in the improper singular—

"—— thou rose-lipped cherubim!"

Everybody knows it is not Hebrew; but then it *is* English; and if it "is not in accordance with *present usage*," it was in accordance with the usage of such men as Bishop Andrewes in 1611, and was part of the version in 1816. Why sweep away these Bible roughnesses, which are full of strength, if not of the trimness and precision which belong to modern pedantry?

The use of the *O* for the sign of the vocative, and of the form *Oh* for that of the optative, appears judicious and admissible; but one word more may be said of the rules as to *a* or *an*. The *h* in *humble* (Prov. xvi. 19) is pronounced silent *h* according to the scheme of the Committee, for they retain the *an*. Though it was there before, it proved nothing in the old Bibles, because no such law was adopted by the translators, who use *an* before the aspirate, as in the instances, *an harlot, an house, an hairy man*. But from the Society's Bible we learn that the *h* in *humble* is silent; so that they have endorsed a mere *cockneyism*, which, though tolerated by some orthoepists, is not the usage of educated Englishmen.

We now come to proper names in the old Testament; in which point " the Committee *have not felt themselves authorized* to introduce any change; regarding the great principle of uniformity in the copies as of higher importance." It is to be regretted that this " great principle" has been disregarded in the much more important case of the New Testament. Everybody is aware of the fact, that " the translators did not retain the names of persons already known in the Old Testament,

in the form in which they had thus become familiar."
But I am not so sure that this is "to be regretted."
As a pastor, I have found this fact to furnish the most
ready key to the perceptions of the unlettered, when I
have wished to explain to them the truth that God was
pleased to employ different languages, in conveying the
Gospel, under the Old and the New Law. It is of some
consequence to make the common reader *feel* the Greek
in his New Testament: at least, if any Christian pastor
is persuaded of this, the Bible Society has no right to
Judaize his New Testament, and so decide against him.
I cheerfully concede that in the Greek form of *Joshua*,
which is the familiar name of our Blessed LORD, there
is a difficulty to the ordinary apprehension. Yet in one
instance, it is explained in the margin by the translators themselves; and I have often found the instance
of use, in explaining to a Bible-class the truth that our
LORD condescended to bear the humble human name of
Joshua, and that Joshua was a signal type of his LORD,
in this, as in other particulars. The Græcised proper
names of the New Testament are, in all other cases,
sufficiently plain to be understood by any one intelli-
gently reading the Scriptures, especially with the references; and, for one, I protest against the Hebraized
look, which the novelty gives to one's Testament. I
prefer to see *Sion*, and not *Zion*, in the New Testament,
because the latter form has a territorial and geographical
association. Thus, in that glorious text, "Ye are come
unto Mount Sion," the form *Zion* seems to remove it
from identity with "the heavenly Jerusalem." The

fact is, GOD seems to have provided the Greek, as new
bottles for new wine, and one feels the propriety of its
idioms, where a new and celestial inheritance comes
into view. I am not sorry to meet *Osee*, and *Noe* and
Sara and *Juda*, in the New Testament; for the bare drop-
ping of superfluities seems a symbol of their baptism into the freedom of the New Covenant, and of the "new-
ness of spirit" which has succeeded the *oldness of the
letter*. If a competent authority should place the original Hebrew names *in the margin*, I doubt not, all
would be satisfied ; but the text, *the text*, let us have it
as our fathers left it! Progress is a good thing in
a proper place ; but this sewing of a new patch here
and there, on "raiment of wrought gold," must strike
sensitive minds as a species of sacrilege.

As to the *italic words*, the Committee seem to have
dealt wisely ; and so, perhaps, with regard to the *parenthesis*. Yet, in sweeping out such a parenthesis as occurs in Rom. v. 13—17, there is "force of commentary"
at least on the version in common use in 1816. In
Gal. i. 1, and Rev. ii. 9, the parenthesis is useful, and
its loss will be felt. As to the brackets, I John ii. 23,
I rejoice that they are removed, and the reason is good ;
but I am not sure that the Committee had any more
right to do it, than they would have to remove the
Park-fence, and open the City-Hall to the approach of
ordinary carriages.

But now we come to the *crux* of the whole affair,
and we are sorry to find it disguised, or at least slurred
over, as a matter of no more moment than the minor

matters among which it is thrown. Why not come out boldly, and say, to begin with, that 'we have altered the received text in *five* very important instances.' Everybody knows that there is no text vital to Gospel truth which may not be evacuated of its sense by the change of a point. The Nicene Creed, itself, evaporates in verbiage, if an iota be inserted in one of its words, and to destroy this iota Athanasius contended against the world, till he had put to flight "the armies of the aliens," and saved the royalties of his Master. Now let every earnest Christian read what follows, and say, even if the Committee be right in their exegesis, whether he is willing to submit such vital matters to the dogmatism of any man, or any set of men, whether they be Popes, Lords, or Brethren! The Bible in common use in 1816 was agreed upon, and the Society's "sole object" was to *circulate* it. The Committee have made divers changes, but they say:

" The following five changes made in the punctuation, are all, *it is believed*, which affect the sense:

(1.)

" Rom. 4, 1. 'that Abraham, our father, as pertaining to the flesh hath found.' Here, according to the order of the Greek, it should read : 'hath found as pertaining to the flesh.' The true pointing, therefore, is a comma after Abraham, and another after father. *This is found in no edition hitherto.*

(2.)

"1 Cor. 16, 22. 'let him be Anathema. Maran atha.' There should be a period after Anathema which no edition inserts. The two words ' Maran atha' are simply an Aramæan formula signifying 'The LORD cometh;' compare Phil. 4, 5.

(3.)

" 2 Cor. 10, 8–11. *All the copies* now have a colon after v. 8, and a period after v. 9, connecting the two verses in sense. The true pointing, however, is a period after v. 8, and then a colon after v. 9 and also v. 10; thus connecting v. 9 as protasis with v. 11 as apodosis. So Chrysostom, and so the Syriac and Latin versions; and this is required by the logical sequence.

(4.)

" Heb. 13, 7. Here should be a period at the end of the verse after ' conversation.' So the translators, the Oxford, and other copies. The Edinburgh and American have sometimes a colon, and sometimes a comma.

(5.)

" Rev. 13, 8. Here a comma is inserted after ' slain;' since the qualification ' from the foundation of the world' refers not to ' slain,' but to ' written;' as is shown by the parallel verse, Rev. 17, 8. The translators wrongly insert a comma after ' Lamb;' others put no stop at all."

Now any changes which *affect the sense*, are changes which no private person has a right to make in the Standard Bible ; yet here the whole *gravamen* is coolly acknowledged: *habemus confitentem reum.* Let us examine the new Bible, and see what becomes of our old faith. (1.) As to Rom. iv. 1, everybody will respect the criticism as such, and take it for what it is worth. But are there not hundreds of texts which might be treated similarly, if such criticism is to intrude into our standards, and not to confine itself to professed commentaries ? A certain Dr. Conquest lately made himself notorious as a conqueror, taking the Scriptures by storm, and publishing a " Bible with 20,000 emendations." The new " Baptist Version," too, has been enough laughed at; but where is the full stop to come, if we begin to deal thus with commas? How cool is the remark of the Committee, after laying down the law as to the true pointing—" This is *found in no edition*, hitherto!"

(2.) The next case is a very serious one. It might do very well in a professed commentary; though even there it would be contradicted, and grammarians would still keep up the litigation. For one, I don't believe it is correct, and if " no edition inserts the period," what right h ,e the Committee to put it there? It is the opinion of some that the formula *Anathema Maranatha* might be rendered "Let him be accursed *when* the LORD cometh." If such be wrong, it is not the Committee's business to alter the text, and decide against them. The Vulgate pointing is a comma before *Maranatha.* Let the reader recur to the language of the Committee and see whether there is no "note or comment" in this pontifical " Anathema."

(3.) In the next case the Committee plead the Latin, because it happens to be with them; but we have seen that it is of little moment when it is against them. Let us allow that the pointing is justifiable, critically. They own that " all the copies" read otherwise. Have they any authority to *introduce* the Vulgate pointing, on critical grounds, into the English Bible?

(4.) In the next case, though, for one, I have been taught to read the text as restored, it is a favourite and a very important passage with many divines who

6

are accustomed to read it otherwise. Such will not thank the Committee for abridging their liberty by a change which may be regarded as at least unnecessary; but they claim the original edition, and if equal judgment had been always observed, in their changes, no one could have censured them.

(5.) But the next instance will shock every Evangelical believer. Will it be believed that the Committee have ventured to tamper with the great beauty and force of Rev. xiii. 8, so as to take away the devotional and doctrinal use of it, forever, and to leave us no such text as "THE LAMB SLAIN FROM THE FOUNDATION OF THE WORLD?" They not only insert a comma after *slain*, to divide it from what follows, but dogmatically pronounce that what follows does not belong to "the Lamb slain," but only to the names of his followers!

They justify themselves by a reference which proves nothing against the received text, in this case, for every Bible student knows how many and rich are the varieties even in the coincidences of Scripture. They presume to say, moreover, that "the translators *wrongly* insert a comma after Lamb." If this is not "going behind the translators," and shoving them into the ditch, besides, I know not how to characterize it. The Vulgate sustains the old pointing—*quorum non sunt scripta nomina in libro vitæ Agni, qui occisus est ab origine mundi.* Few texts are dearer to the devout, and it is a proof text with theologians. Bishop Pearson cites it twice in his work on the Creed. "As he was *the Lamb slain from the foundation of the world*", says he, "so all atonements which were ever made, were only effectual by His Blood." Besides, the same thing is said by St. Peter, (I Pet. i. 20,) who speaks of "the precious blood of CHRIST, as of a Lamb without blemish and without spot, who verily was foreordained before the foundation of the world." How indelicate the assumption, which forbids us to understand St. John, as repeating the same truth, when he uses almost the same words! The text is one which reflects a glorious light from the last pages of Scripture up to the first, and defines JESUS CHRIST as the alpha and omega of the Bible. The altar of Abel, and the sacrifice of Abraham, in Genesis, are thus identified with the Lamb of the Apocalypse; and the text, as received, adds significance to the passage in which we read of the "Song of Moses and the Lamb." I greatly misconceive the amount of devout affection to this time-honoured Scripture, which exists among American Christians, and among the members of the Society itself, if this perversion of the Word of GOD, will be patiently submitted to.

The operation of the Society's rule as to capitals is not always more happy. In three instances out of four, which are given in the Report, there seems nothing to object to, but the last touches a point of vital importance to orthodoxy. In Rev. iv. 5, the Committee have reduced the capital letter of the text, denoting the uncreated Spirit, to a small *s* denoting something inferior. The "seven Spirits of GOD" is but another name for the

Spirit, whose gifts are sevenfold, as we learn from Isaiah. The great proof of the Trinity, which resides in the formula of Baptism, and in the benediction of St. Paul, is made void, if inferior spirits may be joined with those of the Father and the Son. Such an understanding of the text would go far, moreover, to justify the Romish irreverence, which joins St. Michael and St. Mary with the blessed Trinity, in devotional acts. If the seven Spirits be but Angels, and a blessing comes from them (to the exclusion of the Holy Spirit,) when the Father and the Son are both named, the conclusion is inevitable that the Son also may be an inferior spirit, or that the name of St. Michael may be coupled with His, without confusion, or idolatry. The Baptists have already objected to this extraordinary change, in words not to be gainsayed. "The Society's interpretation of the term" say they " weakens and darkens the sublimest formula of benediction to be found in Scripture." Undoubtedly it does, for the Society has not left the small letter to itself, but dressed it out with significance. A small letter was used by the translators, but they had no rule about it, and it tallies with the small letter in the parallel passage of Isaiah. The Bible in "common use," in 1816, had the capital, however, and after its long use, the change would have been objectionable, at any rate. But when the Society gives a reason for the small s, which makes it interpretative, the change becomes a matter of the most serious character. "The word Spirit, everywhere, is made to begin with a capital when it refers to the Spirit of God as a divine agent ; but not when it denotes *other spiritual beings*, or the spirit of man." Such is their rule, and then follows their instance thus :—

English Copies.	*Corrected.*
Rev. iv. 5. seven Spirits of God.	seven spirits of God.

So then these seven spirits are pronounced to be "*other spiritual beings* than the Spirit of God as a Divine agent, or the spirit of man !" The result is painful. We read, indeed, of "seven other spirits" answering to this description, in St. Matthew, (xii. 45,) but they are the spirits of Satan. And as if this meddling were not enough, we find that it not only destroys the text thus instanced, but goes back to the Old Testament, and disturbs the passage in Isaiah. Let us see: "the Spirit of the Lord shall rest upon him ; the spirit of wisdom and understanding, the spirit of counsel and might, &c." Is. xi. 2. But for the Society's rule, there is nothing to object to, in this place. The Spirit of the Lord is first named in His person, and then in His operations; and the small *s* detracts nothing from His Divinity or power. But, as printed under the Society's rule, the reader is informed that "the Spirit of the Lord" is one thing, and the "spirit of wisdom" another! All these spirits, with a small *s*, "denote *other* spiritual beings or the spirit of man !" Was confusion ever worse confounded ?

I submit it to the judgment of devout and reasonable men, whether, at any time, the intrusion of such novelties into a standard, on mere individual responsibility, is not most dangerous. But if, at any time, more especially at this time, when a great portion of our country is witness to the most alarming theological progress towards the Rationalism of Germany. In New England, all things denote the advance of a thoroughly unevangelical spirit, which has possessed itself of the chief seats of learning, and which is successfully contending with the few old-fashioned representatives of a superior orthodoxy, that are left among the descendants of the Puritans. If the evil spirit has been exorcised from its German haunts, it is evident that it is seeking rest in America. And what was the history of its growth in Germany? The school of Semler was founded on a religious basis, the precise counterpart of that which already exists in our own country: on the basis of just such innovations in recognized standards, as the American Bible Society are now making. And in proof of this, I rejoice to cite an authority which no one will despise; the testimony of the late Professor Patton, my revered preceptor in the University of New York, and a most pious, as well as a most erudite man. Speaking of Semler, some thirty years ago, in a paper which he contributed to the "Biblical Repertory," he says:

"Several causes had been operating, for some years before his appearance, through whose instrumentality the theologians and the philosophers of Germany were predisposed to the cordial adoption, and the industrious application of his principles. We allude to the want which the Protestant Churches experienced of controul over *the wildest and most licentious spirit of innovation;* the loss of respect for their symbolical books, the misguided zeal of the Pietists who maintained that Christianity consisted solely in virtue, and the consequent reaction which produced a philosophical, and even a mathematical, school of theology ; and finally, the disposition to employ this very philosophy to explain away, and soften down the more obnoxious doctrines, and to elevate the unassisted efforts of human reason to a supremacy in matters of religion which it poorly merits."

In a day when the New York Tribune is the Bible of thousands of our countrymen ; when Magnetism is the highest spiritualism of thousands more ; when gigantic elements of evil, which have no name, are visible in our great West; and when the subtleties of Dr. Bushnell represent the better phase of the rationalism of New England, can it be wise to insert the sharp end of the critical wedge into the Standard Bible ? Can even these few alterations of the Scriptures in common use, be looked upon with indifference ?

We come to further improvements. With regard to (II.) THE ACCESSORIES OF THE TEXT, the Committee give notice, at the outset, that they mean to be bold; for they say—" We, here tread on different ground." Everybody will concede this, in a degree. It is different ground; but have the Committee any right to be treading on any ground, from which they are fenced off, by the *sole object* of their Society ? For their emendations of the text, they might plead that a pure text was within their province ; but if the accessories be of the nature of "note and comment," as they proceed to show, they have nothing to do with them, on any pretext, unless it be to throw them all overboard. How can note and comment be radically altered and amended,

without the creation of a new commentary? Let any
one compare the new standard with that of 1816, and
see if the comparison does not furnish the most ruthless
commentary on the latter. The question arises at once,
'what do these changes mean?' and one cannot be
long in finding out that the result, at least, is this, that
the Bible shall not be regarded as meaning anything
definitely and unquestionably: it shall "give an uncer-
tain sound."

As to *marginal readings*, the Society have taken several liberties, which are so petty that one fancies they
have all been introduced to excuse a bold marginal
comment on Acts xii. 4, by which the word "Easter"
is neutralized. It is a *just* comment, and I only object
to it as coming from those who are pledged to give *no*
comment. If they had decorated I Cor. v. 8, "therefore let us keep the feast," with the note — " *i. e.*
Easter," it would have been equally just, but still un-
pardonable: and even if they had improved Rev. i. 20,
"the angels of the seven churches" by adding "*i. e.*
bishops," I should have objected not the less.

It may be imagined that the headings of the chapters
are matter of comparatively small consequence: and as
compared with the Sacred Text, they, undoubtedly, are.
Still, the sanctity of the text makes this accessory very
important. It is neither the hallowed censer, nor the
incense of the sanctuary, but it may be the element that
makes the incense burn, and it should not be "strange
fire." As matter of fact, these headings have come
down to us with our Bible; we have read them there,

ever since we first knew the Holy Scriptures; and any change puts a new face on the old Bible. The new Book is a strange book. Even allowing it to be an improvement—*Nolumus mutari*. The old is good enough; it has satisfied all, for ages; it has satisfied the Bible Society for thirty years; there is no fault to be found with it, as a whole; the few blemishes do not amount even to spots on its bright disc; no one would discover them, unless some wiseacre should take the pains to help him; and all together they constitute no objection to a work so long and so universally approved. And moreover, the altering of these heads makes the Society's Bible a different book from that which the British and Foreign Bible Society is sending through all the world; and the Anglo-Saxon race are no longer reading and loving one and the same book. This is an objection to the whole scheme, which no thoughtful mind will lightly dismiss.

But if any change be objectionable, I conceive that the actual changes introduced by the Society, are almost as evil as any change could be, proceeding from good men, with honest intentions. They consist not in, here and there, an emendation, but in a vast system of alteration, and of thorough substitution, characterized, from first to last, by a debased orthodoxy, rationalistic tendencies, and a general aversion to the evangelical and primitive modes of thought which characterize the old Bible.

To make a few specifications, out of many that might be established, I would instance :—

7

1. The entire exclusion of the words "Christ" and "Church" from the Old Testament headings, and partially from the New.

This is a feature of vast significance. Nothing is more valuable to the ordinary reader, as giving him a clue to the fact that the Old and New Testaments are one Gospel, than the great system which runs through the old headings. In them, Christ is everywhere, from the Psalter to the Apocalypse. In the Society's headings, Christ is nowhere. Even in the New Testament, the old familiar phrases, *Christ's passion, Christ's resurrection* and the like, running along the top of the page, and clustering over the heads of chapters, are generally stricken out. We have, instead, *Jesus is crucified, The resurrection of Jesus.* I know that to a believer this is all the same, for sense; and to him the name of Jesus is the adorable name at which he bows his knee. But it is not the same, by any means, to all for whose evangelizing the Gospel is sent. The Jews are willing to allow that *Jesus* was crucified; but Christ Crucified is what Paul preached unto them as their stumbling-block. The Jews always speak of our Saviour as "Jesus of Nazareth," but it was an old law of theirs, that "if any man did confess that He was Christ, he should be put out of the synagogue." I am sorry to see this law so profoundly reverenced in the Society's Gospel. Let any one compare the old and the new headings, and see how thoroughly the latter are Judaized. "That worthy name by which we are called," the name of Christ, which makes us Christians, seems

to have been peculiarly obnoxious to the Society's critics. A similar taste is fashionable among Socinians.
They name the name of JESUS, as they speak of Con-
fucius or Plato. May GOD save our children from being
taught, in their very Bibles, the irreverence, which led a
Socinian minister, not long ago, to publish a work enti-
tled "JESUS and His biographers," meaning thereby
our LORD and His Holy Evangelists!

It is useless to say that Messiah and CHRIST are all
the same thing. So they are to a believer, and so they
are critically. But practically they are very different.
CHRIST and Christian are words which cannot be sepa-
rated. CHRIST means JESUS of Nazareth, for no one
else has ever borne the name in its Greek form. But
Messiah is indefinite. The Jew has no objection to allow
that the 45th psalm means Messiah : in the eyes of some
Socinians it means Messiah, that is, Solomon, as the
anointed of the LORD. But the old heading, " the Majesty and Grace of *Christ's* Kingdom," is something
which they disavow. Accordingly, they are gratified by
the Society, who make it, " the majesty and grace of the
Messiah." This reconciles the dispute. The sword has
passed through the living child, and of course all parties
will be satisfied! Nay—GOD forbid! The true believer
has instincts that cry out against a compromise that destroys what is dearer to his heart than life, even the
truth of GOD's Word, its spirit as well as its letter.

2. The Report treats us to fifteen specimens of the
changes introduced. We may presume that they are
favourable specimens : yet among them we find as gross

a blunder as could well have been committed by the most careless reader of the Bible. Such a blunder, however, is not only made, but actually exhibited in triumph, as an improvement in the matter of removing what is "quaint, obsolete, and *ambiguous.*" Thus, we have it, then :—

Numbers 3. "The first-born are freed by the Levites."

Correction. "The first-born are *taken instead* of the Levites."

A marvellous correction! since it contradicts the very words of Scripture to which it refers, and the fact, familiar to every Biblical student, nay to every well-informed Christian, that *the Levites were taken instead of the first-born!* Here, surely, we are not reviewing the work of Dr. Turner, nor of Dr. Robinson: but how these gentlemen could ever have subscribed their names to such a specimen of *improvement,* and *correction,* may well be matter of surprise. The case would be less flagrant were it not that the errour involves the most profound ignorance of the history of the Levitical tribe, and of the origin of its sacerdotal character. This freeing of the first-born, by the Levites, was a solemn anticipation of the Great Melchisedec, as the first-born of Mary, by which it was provided that he should not be a priest of the Law, but should "pertain to another tribe, of which *no man* gave attendance at the altar." Now we are far from believing that there are many such blunders; but, if, out of fifteen *specimen* corrections, we find one making such mischief with Scripture as this, what confidence can be given to the rest of the work; or to the assurance that among 24,000 variations recorded by the

Collator, "there is not one which mars the integrity of the text, *or affects any doctrine* or precept of Scripture?"

3. If there be a book of the Old Testament which should be always guarded by somewhat of note or comment, it is unquestionably that of the Canticles; and one would have supposed that the Society would have congratulated itself on the possession of a modicum of comment, in its old summaries, to which no one could object, and which served the important purpose of chastening the imagination of all, and checking the irreverence of the profane, by identifying the Canticles with the Apocalypse, and with the 45th psalm, as referring to the Heavenly Bridegroom, and to "the Bride, the Lamb's wife." But alas! certain German critics have found that all this is fiction; that the poem is a mere epithalamium, and celebrates the loves of Solomon, and the Queen of Sheba, or the daughter of Pharoah; that it has little claim to a place in the Canon, and should be exploded as the source of texts for sermons. Archbishop Leighton thought differently. He saw CHRIST in Canticles i. 3, and doubted not that his is the name which is "as ointment poured forth." I rejoice to observe that the Committee disavow any submission to these disciples of Elymas. But while their own convictions are the contrary, is it not amazing that they should have consented to surrender to such critics all that could have been demanded by the worst of them? They have stripped the book of the accessories, that identified it with CHRIST: and they have furnished it with such as sensualize and degrade it. Let the So-

ciety's own Bibles be compared, the old with the new, and let the reader decide, as to the meaning of the change, as a commentary on the "Standard" as it stood before.

SOCIETY'S OLD BIBLE.	SOCIETY'S NEW BIBLE.
Cap. i.	*Ib.*
The Church's love unto CHRIST. She confesseth her deformity—and prayeth to be directed to His flock. CHRIST directeth her to the Shepherds' tents : and shewing His love to her, giveth her gracious promises. The Church and CHRIST congratulate one another.	The bride commendeth her beloved, and inquireth where he feedeth his flock. His answer. Their mutual love.
Cap. ii.	*Ib.*
The mutual love of CHRIST and His Church. The hope and calling of the Church. CHRIST's care of the Church. The profession of the Church, her faith and hope.	The graces of the bride and her beloved, and their delight in each other. He inviteth her to behold the beauties of spring. His care of her. Her trust in him.
Cap. iii.	*Ib.*
The Church's fight and victory in temptation. The Church glorieth in CHRIST.	The bride's despondency. The splendour of the beloved.
Cap. iv.	*Ib.*
CHRIST setteth forth the graces of the Church. He showeth His love to her. The Church prayeth to be made fit for His presence.	The beloved setteth forth the graces of the bride. His love for her. Her desire for His presence.
Cap. v.	*Ib.*
CHRIST awaketh the Church with His calling. The Church having a taste of CHRIST's love is sick of love. A description of CHRIST by His graces.	The Beloved in His garden. The bride's love for Him. His graces described.

Cap. *vi.*

The Church professeth her faith in CHRIST. CHRIST showeth the graces of the Church, and His love towards her.

Ib.

The bride's confidence in the beloved. He setteth forth her graces, and his love for her.

Cap. *vii.*

A further description of the Church's graces. The Church professeth her faith and desire.

Ib.

The bride's graces further described. Her invitation to the beloved.

Cap. *viii.*

The love of the Church to CHRIST. The vehemency of love. The calling of the Gentiles. The Church prayeth for CHRIST's coming.

Ib.

The delight of the bride and her beloved in each other. Love strong as death. The bride's desire in behalf of her sister. She longeth for the coming of her beloved.

Now if some irreverent caviller had taken out his pencil, and written opposite to the old summary, as above, would not everybody have felt that he had made a mockery of it? In my opinion, the Society has furnished such persons with a mockery to begin with. At any rate, there is no CHRIST here ; and we say, with St. Augustine, "if CHRIST be not tasted in the Old Testament Scripture, it hath no savour at all."

4. It is astonishing how, uniformly, they "have taken away the key of knowledge." Even in Isaiah, "the Evangelical prophet," the Committee seem afraid to allow that CHRIST is the sum and substance of his song. To omit the other prophets, then, let us take Isaiah :

SOCIETY'S OLD BIBLE.

Cap. *ii.*

Isaiah prophesieth the coming of CHRIST's kingdom.

SOCIETY'S NEW BIBLE.

Ib.

The future prosperity of Zion.

Cap. *iv.*	*Ib.*
CHRIST's kingdom shall be a sanctuary.	The future prosperity of Zion.

In the next instance we have the famous promise of the SAVIOUR quoted by the Evangelist, S. Matt. (i. 23,) and here we might fairly hope to be indulged with the old heading.

Cap. *v.*	*Ib.*
Ahaz having liberty to choose a sign, and refusing it hath, for a sign, CHRIST promised.	Ahaz refuseth to ask a sign. The LORD promiseth Immanuel.

This amounts to the same thing, with believers; but my readers will recollect that the prophecy is made by some critics to have no immediate reference to CHRIST, or to a miraculous conception! In the next instance we have the great prophecy "For unto us a child is born, &c." Surely here we may have the old heading. But no!

Cap. *ix.*	*Ib.*
What joy shall be in the midst of afflictions, by the kingdom and birth of CHRIST.	The coming of Messiah, and the enlargement of His kingdom.
Cap. *xvi.*	*Ib.*
Moab is exhorted to yield obedience to CHRIST's kingdom.	Moab is exhorted to renew his allegiance to the throne of David.
Cap. *xxviii.*	*Ib.*
CHRIST the sure foundation is promised.	In contrast with the refuge of lies, GOD hath laid in Zion a sure foundation.
Cap. *xxxii.*	*Ib.*
The blessings of CHRIST's kingdom.	Blessings promised to Zion.

We now come to that precious chapter in which CHRIST is everywhere so prominent, that it seems almost irreverent to literalize in the least: "The wilderness and the solitary place shall be glad, etc." The old heading reads as if it were dictated by the exulting spirit predicted in the text; but the new, as if it came from one with eyes still unopened, and from a tongue unwilling to sing. The one is "springs of water," the other a "parched ground."

Cap. *xxxv.*	*Ib.*
The joyful flourishing of CHRIST's kingdom.	The future prosperity of Zion described.

In the next instance, we have a favourite passage, quoted by St. Matthew in full, "Behold my servant whom I uphold, etc." (St. Matt. xii. 18.) But still we cannot keep the good, honest old heading.

Cap. *xlii.*	*Ib.*
The office of CHRIST graced with meekness and constancy. GOD's promise unto him. An exhortation to praise GOD for His gospel.	The servant of Jehovah. His character. GOD's promise unto him. An exhortation to praise GOD for his salvation.
Cap. *xlix.*	*Ib.*
CHRIST, being sent to the Jews complaineth of them. He is sent to the Gentiles with gracious promises. GOD's love is perpetual to His Church. The ample restoration of the Church.	The Messiah and the object of His advent. GOD promiseth Him protection and success. GOD's unchanging love to Zion. Her glorious enlargement foretold.

8

The chapter containing—"I gave my back to the smiters," is next instanced:

Cap. *l.*	*Ib.*
CHRIST sheweth that the dereliction of the Jews is not to be imputed to Him, by His ability to save, by His obedience in that work, and by his confidence in that assistance.	The sins of Israel the cause of their sufferings, and not GOD's inability to save. GOD's gifts to the Messiah. His patient endurance of reproach.

In the next instance, we have the noble chapter which concludes with the prophecy, "So shall he sprinkle many nations." Observe how "free redemption" and its ministers, in the old heading, dwindle down to something about a temporal captivity in the new:

Cap. *lii.*	*Ib.*
CHRIST persuadeth the Church to believe His free redemption, to receive the ministers thereof, to joy in the power thereof, and to free themselves from bondage. CHRIST's kingdom shall be exalted.	Zion exhorted to awake and prepare for her deliverance from captivity. The herald of this event seen upon the mountains. The waste places of Jerusalem called upon to rejoice. The people commanded to depart out of bondage. The humiliation and exaltation of the Messiah.

I am glad to say the all-important 53d chapter is better: but the "offence of the Cross" disappears.

Cap. *liii.*	*Ib.*
The prophet complaining of incredulity, excuseth the scandal of the Cross, by the benefit of His passion, and the good success thereof.	The Messiah despised and rejected. His sufferings in our behalf. His meekness, humiliation, and death. The benefits of His passion.

In the instance of "Ho, every one that thirsteth, etc.," the improvement seems to me gratuitous.

Cap. *lv.*	*Ib.*
The prophet, with the promises of Christ, calleth to faith and to repentance. The happy success of them that believe.	A gracious invitation to accept God's abundant mercy in the Messiah. God's word shall prosper.
Cap. *lvii.*	*Ib.*
He giveth evangelical promises to the penitent.	Promises to the humble and contrite.
Cap. *lix.*	*Ib.*
The damnable nature of sin. The covenant of the Redeemer.	The iniquities of Israel have separated them from God. His covenant with His people.
Cap. *lx.*	*Ib.*
The glory of the Church in the abundant access of the Gentiles.	The glory of the Lord upon Zion. The Gentiles shall come to her light.
Cap. *lxi.*	*Ib.*
The office of Christ. The forwardness and blessings of the faithful.	The office of the Messiah. The glorious results of his coming.

The next instance is that of the chapter beginning with—"Who is this that cometh from Edom." Look at the twain:

Cap. *lxiii.*	*Ib.*
Christ sheweth who He is, what His victory over His enemies, and what His mercy toward His Church. In His just wrath He remembereth His free mercy. The Church in their prayer, and complaint, profess their faith.	The Messiah's triumph over the enemies of Zion. A song of thanksgiving to God for His goodness to Israel. The prayer of His people in their affliction.

In the next citation we have, in the old heading, a reference to original sin, which disappears in the new.

Cap. *lxiv.*	*Ib.*
The Church prayeth for the illustration of GOD's power. Celebrating GOD's mercy, it maketh confession of their natural corruptions. It complaineth of their affliction.	The prayer of GOD's people for aid : with confession of their unworthiness. The desolation of Zion.
Cap. *lxvi.*	*Ib.*
The glorious GOD will be served in humble sincerity. He comforteth the humble with the marvellous generation, and with the gracious benefits of the Church. GOD's severe judgments against the wicked. The Gentiles shall have an holy Church, and see the damnation of the wicked.	GOD delighteth in the contrite spirit ; but rejecteth hypocrisy. Comfort and enlargement promised to Zion. An exhortation to rejoice therein. The enemies of Zion to be destroyed. The message of salvation to be sent to all nations, and the fruits thereof. The fearful end of transgressors.

After a careful comparison of these two columns, I do not think the unbiassed reader will hesitate long as to which is fullest of all that is distinctively Christian. The disciples were not called Messianites at Antioch, but they were called CHRISTIANS, and the Jews are willing to acknowledge Messiah, in nearly all these prophecies, but not CHRIST. Will the Gospel then be the gainer when the old Bible disappears from the homes of America, and this new and lifeless redaction is everywhere its substitute ? Will young and old see CHRIST any more clearly, from this elaborate and sweeping reform? Will the drift and scope of Scripture be any more obvious? Will not the spirit which quickeneth, have given place, in many cases, to the letter which killeth?

Now one may fairly take the ground that this literalization is in fact a commentary which obscures and injures the sense. We treat no other poetry in this way, and he who should do so, would be dismissed with derision. Let us take an example from English poetry: the sublime historic Ode of Gray, which is cast into the form of a prophecy of the English State, and the dynasties of its sovereigns; and submit it to the two kinds of treatment which are under review.

> " Weave the warp and weave the woof
>   The winding sheet of Edward's race :
> Give ample room and verge enough
>   The characters of hell to trace.
> Mark the year and mark the night,
>   When Severn shall re-echo with affright
> The shrieks of death through Berkeley's roofs that ring,
>   Shrieks of an agonizing king.
> She-wolf of France, with unrelenting fangs,
>   That tearest the bowels of thy mangled mate,
> From thee be born, who o'er thy country hangs,
>   The scourge of heaven. What terrours round him wait !"

Now for specimens of the two kinds of summary; and let us see which is the most effectual commentary on the text, at least in degrading and stultifying it. The first shall be according to the confessed principles of a poetical *argument:* the latter, on the principle of the Committee, viz: that of sticking to the letter, and to the baldest inferences as to the meaning of the same.

I.	II.
By the figure of weaving a picture in tapestry, the prophet foreshadoweth the history of divers kings. Edward the Second is cruelly murdered in Berkeley Castle. Isabel of France, his adulterous queen, and destroyer, becomes the mother of Edward the Third: whose wars in her native country are seen to be a just retribution. The terrour of his triumphs.	The bard describeth the operation of weaving. The characters of Hell. A king dieth of some painful disease. A she-wolf teareth out the bowels of a he-wolf: and bringeth forth a little wolf. The country is infested with a race of wolves. This is the scourge of heaven, and is pronounced terrible.

Here are the two kinds of summary, the old and the new! I cannot think of anything as likely to be answered to this, save that I have made sport of the matter. To such an objection, I will borrow a reply from Bishop Lowth, whom I am not ashamed to have copied in the legitimate use of ridicule. In exposing Bishop Hare's system of Hebrew metres, he says: "You may possibly tell me that instead of confuting the Bishop's system, I have made a joke of it, and turned it into ridicule. All the apology which I shall offer upon this occasion, if any be thought needful, is this: that if an object, by being placed in a proper, a just and a true light, appears ridiculous, he who so placeth it, is not to be blamed; the fault is not in him, but in the object itself."

The poet Gray, "were he living at the present day," would certainly be little thankful to any one, who, under the pretext of zeal for the beggarly letter of his Ode, should so degrade its spirit. But how much more would the prophet Isaiah lament any treatment of his argument which should disguise, or make less obvious, the fact that " he testified beforehand the sufferings of CHRIST, and the glory that should follow!" And are the words of the HOLY GHOST to be treated with a sort of commentary, which would degrade an English Pindaric? Is the SPIRIT of GOD, in the Canticles, to be exhibited as portraying the languishments of a carnal love, or the attractions of an earthly bride, when He uses such imagery to depict the marriage of the Lamb? Is the Committee afraid to take the ground that "the testimony of JESUS is the spirit of prophecy?" And if such be the spirit of Isaiah and the Canticles, on what principle do they cast out the old summaries which recognize it, and introduce a flat and senseless literalization which ignores it, thoroughly? I leave the parallel treatment of Gray, to the candid comparisons of the reader, in reviewing their summaries of the Psalms, and the prophets. CHRIST says: "they testify of him;" but, it will be hard for the unlearned reader of the Committee's " Song of Songs," to discern CHRIST in it, through their glasses and glosses, as contrasted with what has been set aside. In a word, St. Cyprian might seem to have written the old summaries, and Paul of Samosata the new: or at least the former might be fairly attributed to " Cocceius, who saw CHRIST everywhere," and the latter to " Grotius, who saw CHRIST nowhere."

In an article of the Edinburgh Review, to which reference has already been made, all that can be said, is said, in favour of a thorough revision of the English

A PRAYER,

FOR CHRISTIAN UNITY.

O God, the Father of our Lord Jesus Christ, our only Saviour, the Prince of Peace ; Give us grace seriously to lay to heart the great dangers we are in by our unhappy divisions. Take away all hatred and prejudice, and whatsoever else may hinder us from Godly Union and Concord: that, as there is but one Body, and one Spirit, and one Hope of our Calling, one Lord, one Faith, one Baptism, one God and Father of us all, so we may henceforth be all of one heart, and of one soul, united in one holy bond of Truth and Peace, of Faith and Charity, and may with one mind and one mouth glorify Thee ; through Jesus Christ our Lord. *Amen.*